Shhh... There's a Clydesdale in my closet

Dedications

From the Author

To Dad and Mom- Thank you for helping me see the vision, and then trust the process. You have instilled in me that hard work and a good amount of stubbornness can get you where you want to be in life. I love you, and am forever grateful for you raising me to always dream big.

To my husband- You are my best friend, and without you by my side, life wouldn't be the same. Thank you for walking on this journey with me, for staying by my side through the rough patches, and rejoicing in our successes. Together, we have created a beautiful family and a beautiful life.

From the Illustrator:

My nephews & niece (Cartier, Kashe, Atreyu, Ezra, and Alaska) You keep my inner child alive!

One afternoon, a little girl named Aria was going for a walk in the pasture behind her house with her dog Daisy.

She sat down and opened her book about all the different kinds of horses. Reading out loud she started with Appaloosas, then Belgians, and Clydesdales...

When all of a sudden she heard a "Thump, Thump, Thump" behind her. Then a "wuffle wuffle" came from over the fence. Daisy's head turned to the side and she let out a "woof." When Aria peeked over the fence she came nose to nose with a lost colt!

"Hello!" greeted Aria, as she and Daisy turned their heads toward the sky to look at the massive horse. "Snuffle, snuffle," answered the lonely horse, looking like he didn't have a friend in the whole world. The poor horse had such a sad lost look in his eyes that Aria couldn't possibly leave him.

She turned her book to the page about Clydesdales and read the description. She looked at the horse and asked, "You're a Clydesdale, aren't you?" The giant horse shook his head up and down as if he understood her.

"Goodness, you look so hungry and sad!" said Aria.
"Here, have the rest of my apple."   "Crunch,
slobber, slobber," said the hungry Clydesdale, as
he gobbled up the apple. He started to turn away
when Aria said, "I can't leave you here by yourself.
I will find somewhere to keep you at home!"

"Shhh," said Aria. "Mom is in the garden.
Daisy you're going to have to create a distraction
so we can get into the house."

Grabbing Daisy's ball out of her pocket, Aria threw it into the garden right next to Mom. Off like a flash, Daisy sped after the ball, with dirt and vegetables flying in every direction.

"Hurry!" exclaimed Aria, as she waited for the Clydesdale to follow her up the stairs to her room. "Mom will be coming any second!" They made their way up the stairs and into Aria's room.

The big horse looked around the room in awe. Everywhere he looked he saw horses. Books lined the shelves, posters covered the walls, and her bed was home to a herd of small horses. Swishing his tail happily, Aria could tell he was glad to be there.

"Aria!" Mom called. "Why are there giant hoof prints in our yard?" Aria came running back into the room, pushing the big horse into her closet. "Faster, faster, she's coming!" A few seconds later Mom came in, looking suspicious. The closet door started to creak open, and Aria rushed to close it. "What's going on in here?" questioned Mom.

"Nothing, I just need to clean out my closet, it's getting too full," replied Aria. "So there were giant hoof prints in the yard?" asked Aria, trying to get Mom's attention off the closet door. "Yes, there are. I'm going to go take another look around and then we will have lunch, ok?" said Mom.

"That was close!" whispered Aria. "We need to be more careful." The big horse shook his head in agreement. "For now, you will have to stay in here. Let me take some of my things out of my closet so you have more room." "Aria, lunch time!" called Mom.

Aria pushed the giant horse back in the closet, just as Mom came into the room. "Aria, what is this MESS?!" exclaimed Mom. "Your room is a disaster!" "I was just cleaning out my closet," replied Aria. "Now the door stays shut, see?" "Well, we are going to eat lunch, and then both of us are going to come back here and clean up this mess," said Mom.

Throughout lunch, Aria couldn't sit still. What was she going to do? How was she going to keep Mom from finding out about the Clydesdale in her closet? She strained her ears, listening for any noise that might sound like a giant horse in her closet. "Thump, Thump" came from upstairs. "What was that?" asked Mom, looking up at the ceiling.

"I didn't hear anything," said Aria. "Thump, Thump" came again. "There, just now! That thump thump noise, it sounds like you have a herd of horses up there," said Mom, pushing back her chair from the table. "It's probably just the wind coming through my window in my bedroom," Aria quickly said. "I'll run up and close it."

Aria sprinted up the stairs, just in time to meet the Clydesdale making his way out of her room. "Stop!" whispered Aria. "You have to stay here, Mom is getting suspicious!" "Wuffle, snort," said the Clydesdale, looking amused, with a sock stuck over one ear. "It's not funny!" said Aria. "You're going to get me in huge trouble. You have to be quiet." She put him back in the closet, closed her window, and went back downstairs to finish lunch.

"Ready to clean up that room?" asked Mom. "Do we have to?" replied Aria. "I'm just so tired." She yawned, trying to stall. "Good try, but I'm not buying it. Let's get to it and it will be done before your Dad gets home." Aria didn't know what else to do but follow Mom back upstairs, hoping the Clydesdale had stayed in her closet.

"What in the world?" exclaimed Mom. "Where did all of your clothes go?" Aria hurried into her room, looking around in amazement. They were gone, the shoes and toys were still there, but the clothes were gone! "I... umm... must have put them away quickly when I came to close the window?" stammered Aria. Her mom looked at her, raising an eyebrow.

"You don't sound very sure of that answer, young lady, what is going on?" Aria looked at the ground, her mind racing, trying to come up with an answer to where her clothes had vanished to. All of a sudden came the sound of snoring from her closet. "Zzzz, wuffle wuffle, zzzz, wuffle wuffle."

"Aria Jo, what in the world have you got in your closet?" asked her Mom, as she reached for the doorknob. Aria closed her eyes, waiting for her Mom's reaction. The seconds felt like hours. "What am I going to do? What is Mom going to say?" she thought to herself.

"Well would you look at this," her Mom said in wonder.
There, lying in a nest of Aria's clothes, was the Clydesdale.
"Aria, you have a lot of explaining to do," whispered her
Mom. "I know, but he's all alone and hungry. He followed
Daisy and me all the way home."

Aria's father arrived home shortly after they had found the sleeping Clydesdale. It had been a long day and Aria could tell he was not in the mood for any surprises. "Hi Dad, how was your day? Do you need anything?" Aria asked, hoping to soften him up before Mom told him about the Clydesdale. "I'm glad to be home, what happened here?" Dad answered, raising an eyebrow with suspicion.

"You better go look in your daughter's closet," Mom said, with a smirk starting to form on her face. Slowly Dad got up and made his way up the stairs. Aria and Mom followed behind. Aria could feel her heart pounding in her chest, waiting for Dad's reaction.

"What in the world!" exclaimed Dad. The Clydesdale stood in the middle of Aria's room, looking quite out of place. "Snuffle, snuffle," said the Clydesdale, as he sniffed Dad's hair. "Aria, what is this?" he asked.
"A Clydesdale of course" she answered.

Dad looked at the big horse, first with confusion, then a smile slowly started to form. "I remember my grandpa having this kind of horse on the farm. They were so big, but so friendly. Everyone loved them. One of my favorite memories was riding in the wagon in parades with Grandpa. You know, sometimes he would even let me take the reins and steer the team."

"So...does that mean we can keep him?" asked Aria anxiously.
"How big is he going to get and where are we going to keep him? And just how much does he EAT?" asked Dad.
"I promise I'll take care of him! I'll feed him and brush him, and we have the whole pasture behind the house he can stay in. Daisy and I will play with him everyday."

Mom and Dad looked at each other again and finally Dad said "If he has nowhere to go, then I think we better keep him. But Aria, you remember what you promised just now, and next time an animal follows you home, let's not keep it in your closet, ok?" he asked, chuckling as he removed the sock from the horse's ear. "Sure Dad," smiled Aria as she wrapped the horse in a hug.

The big horse followed her back outside and down to the pasture behind the house. The Clydesdale no longer looked sad. Now when Aria looked in his eyes she saw hope and happiness. The Clydesdale knew he had found his family.

Vocabulary

Appaloosa- a breed of horse known for its spotted coat coloring.

Belgian- a breed of horse known for its strength, gentle temperament and willingness to work.

Clydesdale- a breed of horse known for its intelligent eyes, mammoth height, and docile nature. A fair amount of "feathering"- hair covering their lower legs and hooves- distinguishes them from other breeds.

Coat- the hair covering the horse's body. It can come in many different colors and patterns.

Colt- a male foal

Herd- a large group of animals of one kind, can be wild or domesticated.

Reins- a leather strap attached to each end of the bit, which is fastened to a bridle.

Team- a pair of horses (usually two, but can be more) hitched together to pull a load.

Pasture- land covered with grass and other vegetation that is suitable for animals such as sheep, cattle, and horses, to graze on.

Now that you have read the book....

Find at least one hidden horse shoe shape in every picture!

About the Illustrator -

Cameo shares a home with her Dad, Sister Desi, 4 dogs, 11 cats, and some girbils. Besides book illustrations, she donates her time and art to rescues and paints pets for people. She always dreamed of having a horse.